For Ryder

Text and illustrations © 2016 Chris Tougas

Special thanks to Tiffany Stone

Owlkids Books acknowledges the financial support of the Canada Council for the Arts, the Ontario Arts Council, the Government of Canada through the Canada Book Fund (CBF) and the Government of Ontario through the Ontario Media Development Corporation's Book Initiative for our publishing activities.

Published in Canada by
Owlkids Books Inc.
10 Lower Spadina Avenue
Toronto, ON M5V 2Z2

Published in the United States by
Owlkids Books Inc.
1700 Fourth Street
Berkeley, CA 94710

Cataloguing data available from Library and Archives Canada

ISBN 978-1-77147-143-5 (bound)

Library of Congress Control Number: 2015957720

Edited by: Karen Li
Designed by: Alisa Baldwin

ONTARIO ARTS COUNCIL
CONSEIL DES ARTS DE L'ONTARIO
an Ontario government agency
un organisme du gouvernement de l'Ontario

Canada Council
for the Arts

Conseil des Arts
du Canada

Canadä

Manufactured in Shenzhen, China, in April 2016, by C&C Joint Printing Co.
Job #HO0173

A   B   C   D   E   F

Publisher of Chirp, chickaDEE and OWL
www.owlkidsbooks.com

Owlkids Books is a division of  Bayard
C A N A D A

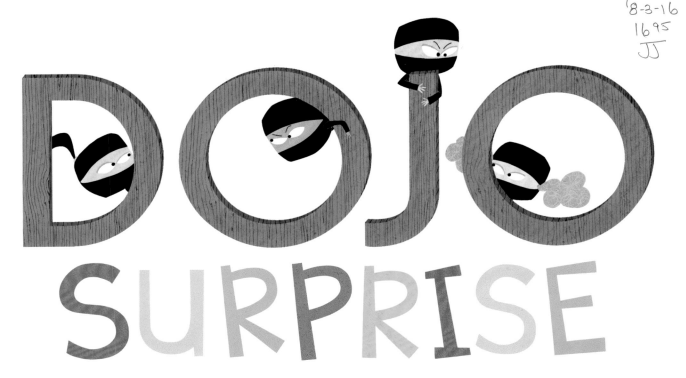

DOJO
SURPRISE

Chris Tougas

Owlkids Books

Little ninja girls and boys
Tiptoe in without a noise,
Early for their dojo day.
Something sneaky's under way.

Ninjas scatter left and right,
Darting, dashing out of sight.
Master calms down from his screaming,
Wonders, *Was I only dreaming?*

It's a total dojo scare!
Master must be more aware.
"If I use my ears and eyes,
I won't be taken by surprise."

Ninjas scurry past the Master.
Hurry, hurry! Faster, faster!
Ninjas weave between the beams
When—

SPLITTER!   SPLAT!

the Master screams...

Master spots a purple pool
And worries that it's...*dragon drool!*
While Master's frozen stiff with fear,
The little ninjas disappear.

It's a total dojo scare!
Master must be more aware.
"If I use my ears and eyes,
I won't be taken by surprise."

Ninjas work in tiny teams
When—

Ninjas perch in hiding places.
Master's poor heart pounds and races.
Putting ninja pride aside,
Master finds a place to hide.

It's a total dojo scare!
Master must be more aware.
"If I use my ears and eyes,
  I won't be taken by..."

Master gasps, then laughs and cries.
He can't believe his ninja eyes!
Streamers, poppers, candles, cake—
Little ninjas sure can bake!

Master's given quite a lift!
A birthday party—what a gift!
"Make a wish!" the ninjas shout
As Master blows the candles out.

The little ninjas give a bow.
Master bows and whispers,

They make a toast and drink some punch,
Then cut the cake and MUNCH, MUNCH, MUNCH!

Ninjas play a party song.
Master grins and grooves along.

All is cool—or so it seems,
When suddenly...

A GAGGLE OF GEESE

The Collective Names of the Animal Kingdom

Atheneum Books for Young Readers
An imprint of Simon & Schuster Children's Publishing Division
1230 Avenue of the Americas
New York, New York 10020

Graphic design by Design/Section
The text of this book is set in Bodoni Book
First edition
Printed in Singapore by Tien Wah Press (Pte) Ltd.
10 9 8 7 6 5 4 3 2 1
Library of Congress Cataloging-in-Publication Data is available.
ISBN 0-689-80761-9

A Gaggle of Geese

The Collective Names of the Animal Kingdom

PHILIPPA-ALYS BROWNE

ATHENEUM BOOKS FOR YOUNG READERS

A gaggle of geese gathering

A skulk of foxes slinking

A set of badgers blathering

A parliament of owls winking

A knot of toads scrambling

A rookery of penguins stooping

A drove of pigs ambling

A flight of butterflies swooping

A charm of finches flirting

A pride of lions lazing

A gam of whales squirting

A herd of zebra grazing

A shoal of mackerel flickering

A cluster of cats romping

A colony of squirrels snickering

A mob of kangaroos stomping

A leap of leopards jumping

An army of ants following

A crash of rhinos thumping

A pod of hippos wallowing

A murder of crows scheming

A pack of dogs racing

A sloth of bears soon dreaming

A troop of monkeys chasing

A swarm of bees buzzing in the sun

A down of hares – see how they run!

Notes

Where do the collective names of animals come from? The ones listed in this book are just a few of many such names, most of which have been in use since the fifteenth century or earlier. The first written record of collective names for animals is *The Egerton Manuscript*, which dates from about 1450. When William Caxton introduced the printing press to England in 1476, one of the first books he printed was *The Hors, Shepe & The Ghoos*, which also listed the collective names of animals. But the most comprehensive listing was in *The Book of St Albans*, which dates from 1486.

Why are there so many collective names in English for different groups of animals? One answer may be that, in the past, animals played a more integral part in people's lives than they do today. Agrarian cultures valued many species for the food they produced, as we do, but also for the many practical uses of their hides and fur, and for the work they helped to accomplish. People working on the land often watched the behavior of animals because it could convey important information. For example, cows often lie down when they sense that rain is coming, long before any clouds have appeared in the sky. Finally, throughout the world hunting has been a vital part of survival for many cultures, and a good hunter needs to observe closely both the behavior of the animal he hunts and the movements of its prey.

While many of the collective names of different animal groups reflect the animal's behavior, some are more simply descriptive. Some are both: for example, "a knot of toads" at once describes their behavior during the mating season and their knobbly appearance. Other collective names have become useful in describing people as well as animals. For example, we say "a skulk of thieves" in addition to "a skulk of foxes."

Other collective names describe animals in a way that no longer typifies their behavior in relation to humans. For example, we no longer see pigs being driven on foot along country lanes to the local market, as our grandparents might have done, so "a drove of pigs" may sound strange to us.

There are no hard and fast rules about the collective names of animals, but we can classify them into four groups:

Appearance. The collective name describes the appearance of the animal – e.g., "pride" conveys the regal bearing of a lion.

Characteristic. The collective name describes a distinctive behavioral trait of the animal – e.g., "leap" describes how a leopard jumps on its prey.

Habitat. The collective name describes how or where the animal lives – e.g., a "rookery" is the large nesting ground in which penguins gather to breed.

Onomatopoeic. The sound of the collective name describes an aspect of the animal's behavior – e.g., "gaggle" *sounds* like the noise made by geese.

The following notes classify the collective names in this book, and give information about each animal.

A GAGGLE OF GEESE (*Characteristic/Onomatopoeic*)

"Gaggle" describes the cackling sound made by groups of domestic geese. It is also used in the expression "a gaggle of gossips." As well as being valued for their eggs and meat, geese are prized for their feathers, which are used in pillows, insulated clothing, and sleeping bags. In many rural parts of the world, it is still a common sight to see gaggles of geese in farmers' orchards and on village greens.

A SKULK OF FOXES (*Characteristic*)

To "skulk" means to move in a stealthy way, so as to avoid being noticed. Foxes are solitary hunters, who move like this so that they can creep up on their prey without frightening it away. Most foxes feed on mice, voles, rabbits, chickens, birds' eggs, large insects, and carrion.

A SET OF BADGERS (*Habitat*)

Badgers are nocturnal animals that live in groups in deep underground chambers on hillsides or in forests. These chambers are known as "sets." Many of them are used by successive generations of badgers.

A PARLIAMENT OF OWLS (*Characteristic*)

The word "parliament" comes from the Middle English and French word *parler*, which means "to speak." Owls are nocturnal birds of prey with very distinctive calls. The owl's call, and its reputation for wisdom, may account for this collective name.

A KNOT OF TOADS (*Appearance/Characteristic*)

Toads are amphibious animals. They can be distinguished from frogs by the roughness of their skin and by their shorter hind legs. They are usually brownish grey in color with a warty skin, flat head, and swollen glands above the ears, giving them a "knotty" appearance. During the mating season, clinging groups – "knots" – of toads can be seen covering the surface of ponds.

A ROOKERY OF PENGUINS (*Habitat*)

Penguins live in Antarctica, where they gather in large "rookeries" to breed. In the mating season, penguins can be seen hopping, jumping, waddling and tobogganing towards their favorite breeding sites. In many areas, smooth paths have been worn over hard rock by countless generations of birds – penguins always take the same route to their rookery.

A DROVE OF PIGS (*Characteristic*)

For centuries, pigs have been raised for food in almost every part of the world. They were one of the first animals to be domesticated, probably because they have many offspring at a time, grow and mature rapidly, and can scavenge for a wide range of foods. As well as meat, pigs provide leather for luggage and gloves, and their bristles are used in brushes. Until modern times, it was customary to see droves of pigs being driven on foot to the local market.

A FLIGHT OF BUTTERFLIES (*Characteristic*)

A butterfly's life passes through four stages: the egg, larva (caterpillar), pupa (cocoon or chrysalis), and imago (adult). Most adult butterflies fly during daylight hours and can be seen busily seeking nectar from flowering plants. As well as nectar, they feed on pollen, rotting fruit, carrion, dung and urine. Butterflies, and moths make up the second-largest insect order (Lepidoptera).

A CHARM OF FINCHES (*Characteristic*)

Finches are found in the Americas, Eurasia, Africa, Asia, and Australia. Many finches are fine songbirds and are popular as caged birds – especially the canary and its relatives. The sound of the finch's sweet voice probably gave rise to this collective name.

A PRIDE OF LIONS (*Appearance/Habitat*)

Known as the "king of beasts" on account of its proud appearance and regal bearing, the lion once ranged throughout Africa and from Europe as far east as Iran and India. Today Eurasian wild lions are limited to the Gir Sanctuary in India; in Africa, they still roam south of the Sahara. Lions live in a family unit or "pride," which may have between four and thirty-seven members. The females rarely leave the pride, while the male cubs stay until they are expelled by a group of older males. They will then roam about for several years before challenging rival males for the leadership of a pride.

A lion pride may hunt a territory of 13–250 square miles. Both males and females establish their territories by leaving a strong scent on bushes and by roaring to ward off other prides and nomadic males.

A GAM OF WHALES (*Characteristic*)

Whales are unique among mammals in that their entire life cycle, from birth to death, occurs in the water. Whales were heavily hunted in the past, but because of the drastic decline in their numbers, conservationists all over their world are seeking a total ban on commercial whaling. The expression "gam" probably comes from the whale's habit of sporting or "gamboling" in the sea. In the past, when two whaling ships met up at sea (and voyages could last up to three years), it called for a "gam" – a meeting of crews via their whaleboats and the "gamming chair."

A HERD OF ZEBRA (*Habitat*)

The zebra is native to Africa. The smallest species is the mountain zebra, which roams the mountain ranges of South Africa in small "herds." Burchell's zebra, named after the British naturalist William John Burchell, wanders about in large herds in the central and eastern plains of the continent. The largest species, Grevy's zebra, inhabits the arid plains of east Africa and is nearly extinct. Other animals for which "herd" is a collective name include cattle and horses.

A SHOAL OF MACKEREL (*Habitat*)

Mackerel is the common name of forty-eight species of fish sought for food worldwide. Mackerel swim in huge "shoals" near the surface of the sea. They feed on small fish and crustaceans, and spawn in open water during late spring and early summer. Mackerel fishing is an important industry in Great Britain, Norway, Ireland, Canada, and the northeastern United States. "Shoal" is also the collective name for bass.

A CLUSTER OF CATS (*Characteristic/Habitat*)

Cats have long been popular as household pets, as well as being valued for killing mice and rats. Cats have a keen sense of smell and hearing, excellent night vision, and extremely supple bodies. Female cats usually give birth to litters of about four kittens. A "cluster" describes a group of things or objects that grow or live closely together, as is typical among domestic cats belonging to the same household or wild cats hunting in the same group.

A COLONY OF SQUIRRELS (*Habitat*)

The squirrel is a rodent belonging to the same family as the woodchuck, chipmunk, and prairie dog. Squirrels live in all parts of the world except Australia. Apart from ground squirrels, they live mainly in trees and have a diet of nuts, seeds, buds, and occasionally insects. In colder climates, squirrels store a food supply in late summer/autumn and hibernate during the winter months. The origin of this collective name is unknown.

A MOB OF KANGAROOS (*Characteristic*)

Kangaroos are native to Australia and the neighboring islands. Kangaroos are normally timid, but they can be dangerous when at bay, pummelling their attackers with their forepaws and with their strong hind legs. Kangaroos usually move around in big groups, and this may have given rise to "mob" as a collective name.

A LEAP OF LEOPARDS (*Characteristic*)

The leopard inhabits much of Africa and Asia. It is an extremely agile climber and often stalks monkeys up in the trees, hunting mainly at night. When game is scarce, it will also eat field mice, fruit, porcupines, and baboons. Leopards "leap" when they attack their prey.

AN ARMY OF ANTS (*Characteristic*)

Ants of many different species are found across the world in both temperate and tropical countries. All ants live in large, organized groups. Many of them build elaborate nests, with a great network of chambers and galleries beneath stones, logs or underground. Their industrious and precisely coordinated behavior probably gave rise to "army" as a collective name.

A CRASH OF RHINOS (*Characteristic*)

Once widespread, the rhinoceros has now been reduced to five species living in Asia, the Malay Archipelago, and tropical Africa. Rhinos live singly, in pairs, or in small groups. The term "crash" probably comes from the rhino's reputation for being dangerous, but unless provoked, rhinos are usually quite peaceable creatures.

A POD OF HIPPOS (*Appearance/Habitat*)

Hippopotamuses are native to Africa. They spend most of the day in rivers with only their eyes, ears, and nostrils above the surface of the water. During the day they live on aquatic vegetation and at night they come out to feed on land plants. Like peas in a pod, hippos are usually to be found in small groups, though larger groups of up to 150 can occur. Sometimes the term "pod" is also applied to groups of seals and whales.

A MURDER OF CROWS (*Appearance/Characteristic*)

Crows are native to every continent except South America. They are highly intelligent and adaptable and are noted for their ability to thrive near humans. Crows are gregarious birds and at breeding times they can gather in the thousands. The spectacle of many crows massing together in this way is very awesome, and may well be the source of the collective name. "Murder" could also be connected with the tendency of crows to mob owls and other predators in order to defend their territory. In turn, crows may also be mobbed by other birds because they feed on eggs and nestlings as well as on other small animals, vegetable matter, carrion, and rubbish left by humans.

A PACK OF DOGS (*Characteristic/Habitat*)

The domestic dog has been a companion and working partner for human beings since prehistoric times. It is believed to be the direct descendant of the wolf, which once roamed throughout Europe, Asia, and North America. "Pack" is the term used for dogs, such as foxhounds, that hunt in groups. It is also applied to some groups of birds, like grouse.

A SLOTH OF BEARS (*Appearance/Characteristic*)

Bears occur in every continent, except Africa, Antarctica, and Australia. They live in many different habitats, from the Arctic ice to the forests and mountain ranges of more temperate regions. They can roam over great distances in search of food, but during the winter months the black, brown, and polar bears become quite inactive, hibernating for between three and five months. This hibernation period – together with their rather slow, lumbering gait – may be the source of this collective name.

A TROOP OF MONKEYS (*Characteristic/Habitat*)

The three main monkey families are the American monkey, the marmoset monkey, and the Eurasian monkey. Most monkeys live in trees, usually in "troops" of twenty or more individuals. They feed chiefly on leaves, fruits, and insects. The collective name probably arose from the similarity of a group of monkeys to a "troop" of noisy children.

A SWARM OF BEES (*Characteristic*)

There are about 20,000 species of bees in the world, some of which are solitary while others live in organized colonies. Plants are pollinated more by bees than by any other insect, while the honeybee is also valued for the honey it produces. A "swarm" of bees is a group of bees that leaves the hive at a particular season, gathers in a compact group, and, led by the queen bee, fly off in search of a new dwelling place.

A DOWN OF HARES (*Characteristic/Habitat*)

Hares are distributed throughout the world. They prefer to live in places where the soil is loose and dry and where brushwood affords shelter. The origin of this collective name may be connected with the use of "down" to describe the chalk uplands of south and southeast England. Hares feed mainly on herbs, tree bark, and vegetation. During March, they are particularly frisky, emerging at night to box with each other by the light of the full moon – hence the saying "mad as a March hare."